It's Your Turn, Roger!

ALSO BY SUSANNA GRETZ

Roger Takes Charge!
Roger Loses His Marbles!
Roger Mucks In!

A Red Fox Book

Published by Random House Children's Books
20 Vauxhall Bridge Road, London SW1V 2SA

A division of Random House UK Ltd
London Melbourne Sydney Auckland
Johannesburg and agencies throughout the world

Copyright © Susanna Gretz 1985

3 5 7 9 10 8 6 4 2

First published by
The Bodley Head Children's Books 1985

Red Fox edition 1996

The right of Susanna Gretz to be identified as the
author and illustrator of this work has been
asserted by her in accordance with the Copyright,
Designs and Patents Act, 1988.

Printed in Singapore

RANDOM HOUSE UK Limited Reg. No. 954009

It's Your Turn, Roger!

Susanna Gretz

RED FOX

In all the flats in Roger's house
it's nearly supper time.

Roger, it's your turn to set the table.

That's his sister calling.

I see you, Roger!

That's his little brother.

Roger, you know we all take turns at helping.

That's Roger's dad.

That's Roger's mum.

"OK, OK," moans Roger.

"In other families you don't have to help," Roger grumbles.
"Are you sure?" asks Uncle Tim. "Why don't you go and see?"

"All right, I *will*," says Roger.

He stomps out of the door . . .

... and on upstairs.

"Come in, come in," says the family on the first floor.

"Do I have to set the table?" asks Roger.

"Certainly not, you're a guest. Come in and have some fishmeal soup."

What a fancy supper table, thinks Roger . . .

. . . but what *horrible* soup!
"Excuse me," says Roger, and he hops upstairs.

"Come in, come in," says the family on the second floor.

"Do I have to set the table?" asks Roger.

"Certainly not, you're a guest. Come in and have some mud pancakes."

What a messy table, thinks Roger . . .
and what *dreadful* pancakes!

No one notices as he slips out.

"Come in, come in," says
the family on the third floor.
"Do I have to set the table?"
asks Roger.
"Certainly not, you're a guest.
Come in and have a little snack."

This family doesn't even *have* a table . . .

Roots and snails – YUK!
Roger hurries away.

"Come in, come in," says
the family in the top flat.
 "Do I have to set the table?"
asks Roger.
 "Certainly not, you're a guest.
Come in and have some milky mush."
 "Well..." says Roger.
 He *is* getting hungry.

Everyone in the top flat is busy
getting the supper table ready.

Roger sits by himself
and watches.
   If I weren't a "guest",
I could help too, he thinks.

Supper time!

"What's a guest?" he asks someone.
"Well . . . guests don't really live here."
"Oh," says Roger. "Now where *I* live . . ."

Just then a special smell creeps all
the way upstairs to the top flat.

"Where *I* live," shouts Roger, "there's
something *good* for supper –"

"– and it's my turn to help!"

"I took your turn for you," says
Uncle Tim.
"I'll take your turn tomorrow,"
says Roger, between mouthfuls.

Worm pie for dessert – whoopee! Roger's favourite.